Lily Takes A Walk
Satoshi Kitamura

Happy Cat Books

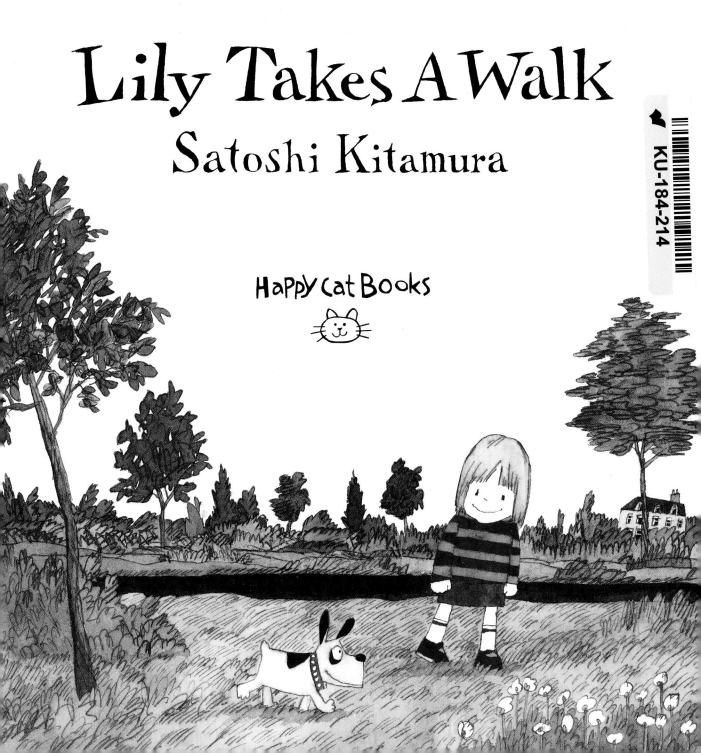

Lily likes going for walks with her dog, Nicky.

Sometimes they walk for hours and hours
until the sun starts to slip down
behind the hill.

Even if it begins to get dark on the way home,
Lily is never scared because
Nicky is there with her.

Today she does the shopping
for her mother and then . . .

she stops for a moment
to look at the evening star.
'Look, Nicky,' she says.
'That's called the Dog Star.'

As Lily walks past Mrs Hall's
window, she waves.
Mrs Hall is always knitting.

Bats flitter and swoop in the evening sky.
'Aren't they clever, Nicky?' says Lily. 'Not far, now.'

She stops by the bridge to say goodnight
to the gulls and the ducks on the canal.

Soon, she comes to the last corner.
This is the best moment of all. She can see
the light in her window and smell her supper cooking.

Lily's mother and father always like to hear
what she has seen on her walk.

Before long, it is time for bed.
Nicky is already in his basket.
'We had a good walk today,
didn't we?' says Lily.
'Goodnight, Nicky.
Sleep well.'